LITTLE COTTON HEART

Flori Paquette

Author's Tranquility Press
COLLEGE PARK, GEORGIA

FLORI PAQUETTE / Author's Tranquility Press
2300 Camp Creek Parkway Ste 120 #1255
College Park, GA 30337
www.authorstranquilitypress.com

Ordering Information:
Quantity sales. Special discounts are available on quantity purchases by corporations, associations, and others. For details, contact the "Special Sales Department" at the address above.

LITTLE COTTON HEART / FLORI PAQUETTE
Hardback: 978-1-966088-37-0
Paperback: 978-1-966088-38-7
eBook: 978-1-966088-39-4

Table of Contents

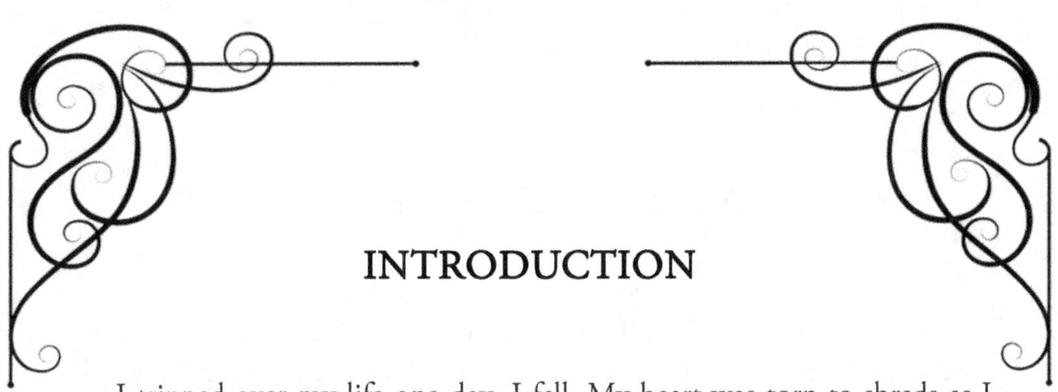

INTRODUCTION

I tripped over my life one day. I fell. My heart was torn to shreds as I landed hard in a mind that was a stranger to me. I found myself in a confusing descent, as I became aware of pieces of myself I never knew existed. The pain seemed unbearable. I can remember lying on the floor, begging God to help me. Little did I know that what I was experiencing was only the beginning of a very long, arduous, season of tribulation.

It felt like I was in a tempestuous ocean storm. Writing was my way of blowing into my desire to keep my head up. It's how I kept breathing and held onto my place in this world. This little book is some of what I wrote as I passed through all it took to find a solid sense of self and the ability to feel whole, happy, and at peace with God.

I would not have found some of my life's most valued treasures, nor would I know how deep the refreshing waters of healing could run, if I had not endured far beyond what I believed to be my capacity. I found buried treasures as I tasted dusty gravel and fell into waters that were well over my head.

Thoughts of ending my grief entered my mind from time to time. My husband and children kept me alive by just being who they are to me. I could not give up on them. I am truly grateful to them for bearing through it with me.

I want to encourage those who are navigating through their own lonely abyss to grasp onto their desire to find the light, and then refuse to let go. Joy comes in the morning to those who endure through the cold of night. My light was in the hope of finding it until I could feel it warm my shoulders and glow in my heart.

ACKNOWLEDGMENT

I thank the Lord for His life-transforming grace. He walked me through much more than I could take. When I couldn't hold on, He never let go. He showed me that He understands because He healed me in ways only God could have known I needed.

I have infinite love and gratitude for the man who has stood on the ground faithfully, holding the string that kept me from being captured by the high winds of dissociation and carried away to worlds unknown. He stayed by my side and made sure that I had the very best of everything, all through the life we have shared together; the father of my children; and my husband, Don.

I want to give honor to my therapist. He always found a way to light a candle when it was too dark for me to see. He believed in me when I couldn't believe in myself. He caught me when I fell off the edge many times. Phil is a gifted therapist and a godly man. He held on tight until I was ready to let go.

My dear Sally; traveled with me through all the confusion and the pain, just to hold my hand. She gave me a shoulder to cry on and a wall to throw eggs at. Sally was faithful in prayer and a spiritual mentor. I treasure her memory.

To my kindred spirit Penelope, is proof of God's understanding and care for things residing deep in my heart. I have no idea how I would have made it through the woods without her compassion, support, and hilarious sense of humor. We belly-laughed through the darkness.

I am grateful to those who tried to understand but couldn't. I spent a lot of time not being able to understand as well. Because of them, I discovered what it is to have solitude, in the experience of feeling isolated and misunderstood.

Turn, Run

Turn, run,
from the beating of the drum.
Make my body become numb.

Block it out,
Cover my ears,
so I will not feel the tears.

Run, run,
Stay far away.
Move on, press on, another day.

Don't listen.
Don't dance.
Don't let my heart romance.

Keep my eyes away; can't bear to look
For what I see,
I may not be.

There is no room.
There is no time.
The truth within me is a crime.

I must conform.
I cannot be
that person who is truly me.

I write it out,
My heart's desire,
then turn and burn it up with fire.

There is no room.
It's not the pace.
So throw it in the fireplace.

After the ashes
have grown cold,
I feel my heart grow sad and old.

Live the other life I see.
The one I force,
and learn to be.

I must dance
to someone else's song.
So why is mine so very wrong?

My body, my energy,
is what is needed.
My heart, I fear, will not be heeded.

Not as smart, is what I fear.
So I go on and play the part.
Ignore the pounding of my heart.

I know how
to make myself be
almost anything, then call it me.

What is your wish?
What is your pleasure?
I'll give it to you in full measure.

I hide the truth,
can't let you in.
I'm so afraid you'll call me sin.

That's rejection
I can't face.
So, I keep trying to run the race.

I don't fit.
I can see,
there is no room for the real me.

I've been hurting
for so long,
because I cannot sing my song.

I've tried to toss my heart away.
Now I must face it,
in some way.

Now, dear God,
where to from here?
I must find a way to conquer fear.

God Will Be Glad And I Will Be Pretty

I am just a lost girl. Don't stare at me because I don't have any clothes. Please, don't touch me. My skin is very sore and some of my dirt may rub off on you. Then you will run away from me!

Stand far away from me. I have lots of germs. You wouldn't want to catch what I have. It feels awfully bad.

Don't try to pull me in to wash me off, so you can dress me in your clothes. Don't try to make me wear your perfume. There is a reason why I'm naked.

You see, some people found me wondering when I was looking for a home. They took me to live at their house. They told me it was God's.

"Take off your clothes," they said to me. They told me that my clothes made God sad. I didn't want to make God feel bad, so I gave the all the pretty things I wore. All the people stood around and stared at me. They looked closely at all my skin. After that, they brought me other things to wear. I didn't want to put them on. I could tell they were made for someone else, but they told me God said they made me pretty. I wanted God to think I was pretty.

I had to wear those clothes all the time. They pinched and rubbed so much; they made me bleed. They made it hard for me to breathe.

The house looked very pretty for all who passed by. It was clean in front. It was covered with thick, white paint. The yard was full of flowers and fruit trees. People who walked by looked at the flowers and said we had a beautiful garden. We would give them fruit from the trees in the front yard because the backyard had yucky fruit with lots of worms.

Inside the house, there was a special place. We saved it for people who came to visit. In that place, the curtains were kept wide open. It was always bright and warm. We had to work very hard to keep it clean. There were lots of pretty things to look at. We dusted and polished them all the time just in case someone came to spend some time with us.

All the rest of the house was different. We had to keep the doors locked and all the curtains shut tight. We were forbidden to open them unless the master gave the order. If someone did, they got in lots of trouble. The master said we must obey the rules to keep us safe from bad people who tried to tell us they were good.

On the inside of the doors that locked, it was dark, and I thought it smelled bad. Everybody else said there was something wrong with my nose. They said it smelled just the way it should, so I believed them.

The master of the house said he was good. He said he knew the voice of God. He said it was wrong to think bad things about him because it would make God mad. He told me that I would get hurt and die if I ran away. I felt sick to my stomach most of the time because I had to try so hard not to think terrible things about him.

I watched people get in awful bad trouble when they got mad at the master. He would get other people to beat them with mean words that made them cry until they said sorry. I got beatings too when I got mad. It hurt me. I cried and cried until I couldn't remember how to think like myself anymore.

I always wanted to run away, but I was too afraid. They told me invisible monsters would attack me. The monsters growled inside my head. I thought they would kill me, or people who I loved. The monsters would

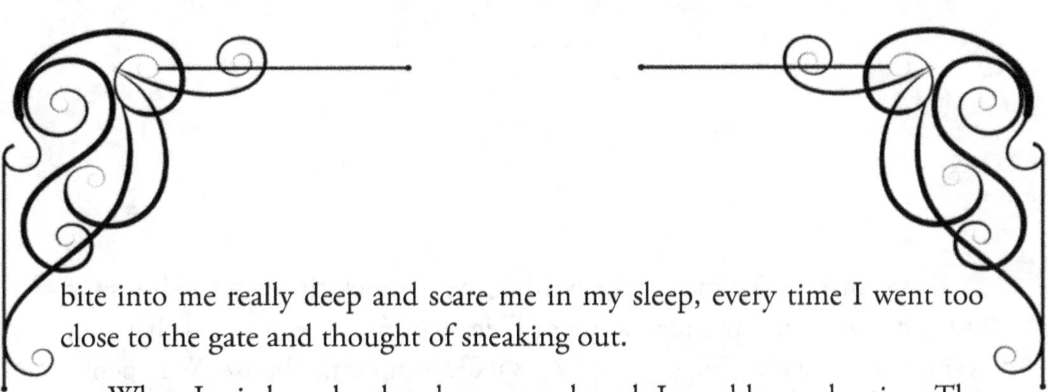

bite into me really deep and scare me in my sleep, every time I went too close to the gate and thought of sneaking out.

When I cried too loud and someone heard, I would get a beating. The monsters would hear my quiet tears and bite me for being bad. I learned to stop crying. That's when I looked in the mirror and saw someone else look back at me.

One day, something different happened. The master opened a little window in the dark part of the house. Everybody saw the light and got up close to it. The sun came in and it felt very good. It was very nice to sit by the little window. The sun felt warm on my sore skin. The air smelled fresh and sweet. We could sit there if we wanted to because the master said that it was good.

Then my nose wanted me to open another window. I thought it would make the house smell better. The monsters started growling and said that they would bite. But my nose got stronger than my fears.

Almost everybody wanted to let the good air in. We started to open tiny cracks in all the windows behind the curtains, so the master wouldn't see. That's when I knew my nose was working just the way it should.

The monsters got loud and bit me every night for being bad. I was very scared. They made me feel all mixed up. I thought that maybe God would tell them to kill me. I cried because the monster bites started to hurt so much. My stomach always burned when I tried to sleep because I was sick from being worried.

I told God that He could kill me if I was bad. I made up my mind to run away. If those were God's monsters, I didn't want to be with Him anymore.

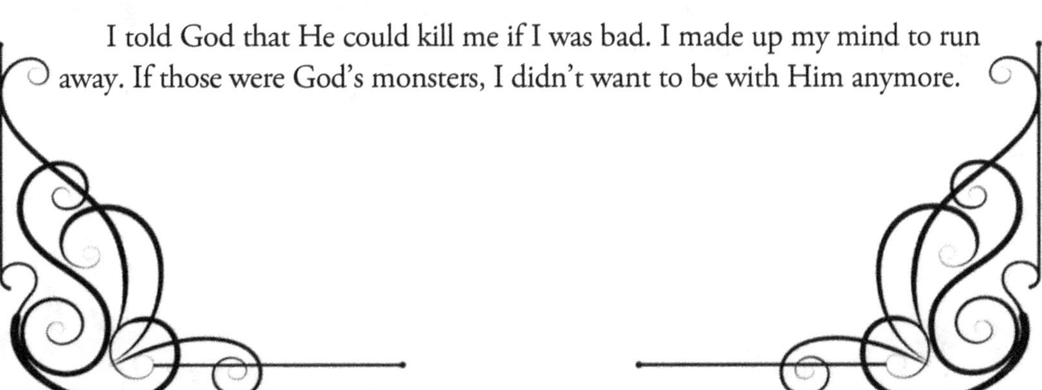

I was mad at the master for beating me. I snuck through the house to say goodbye to my friends. Some of them whispered in my ears that they wanted to leave too. We waited. We walked around the house. We opened the curtains. Light came shining in. That's when we could see all the horrible things that made the house have a stinky smell. We saw cuts and bruises on everybody's skin. I found out that those awful monsters bit everyone. I thought that I was the only one. The master gave beatings to lots of people. He told them never to tell.

After we saw those bad, ugly things, the monsters ran away. There was too much light. They couldn't stay. The master didn't have them to help him hide. He got very scared because we saw all the bad things that he did. He ran out of the house. Some of the people went with him. He hides behind them now.

I helped tear the house apart. I didn't want the master to sneak back in. He could lie to other people who are lost. Then they would get hurt like I did.

For a while, I stayed by the wrecked-up house. Most of the people were there because they didn't know where else to go. We helped each other find our things. We cried and put band-aids on each other.

The time came for me to say goodbye. I took off the clothes they made me wear. It hurt way too much to keep them on. I looked for my old clothes. They were in the dirt, under the front steps. I tried to put them on. It didn't work. They didn't fit me anymore.

I stood on the front steps. My nose sucked up the fresh air. I looked up the road one way and then down the other way. Then I walked through the gate. No monsters growled at me. I didn't get any bites. The warm sun gave my skin a big hug. My heart reached up to hold God's hand. It felt so good.

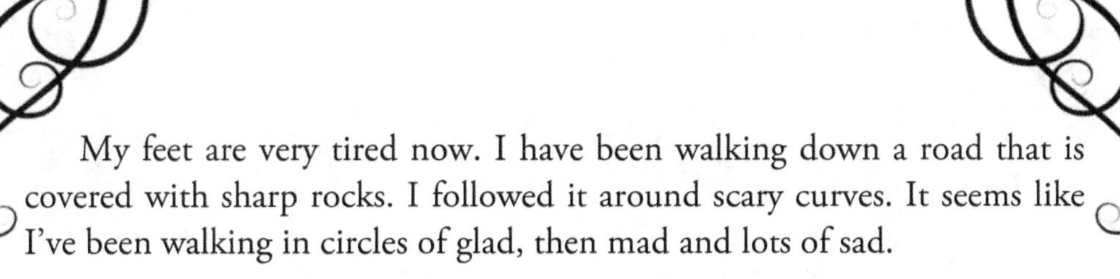

My feet are very tired now. I have been walking down a road that is covered with sharp rocks. I followed it around scary curves. It seems like I've been walking in circles of glad, then mad and lots of sad.

Do not feel sorry for me. God is taking me to His river. I will take a long bath. All the dirt will get washed off. I will lay in the sun, where all the germs will die. My feet will feel better.

When I am ready, I will get up. I will walk naked until I find pieces of clothes that I think look nice on me. I can pick flowers along the way. I can rub them on my skin. That is the kind of perfume I want to wear.

God will be glad, and I will be pretty.

A Place

I need to find a place, where
I can always feel safe.

I need to find a place, where
I can always feel peace; through
turmoil and confusion.

I need to find a place, where
I can sit with my emotions and
listen while they speak.

I need to find a place,
no more than a minute away.

I need to find a place,
I can run to without feet.

I need to find a place, that's
constant here or there.

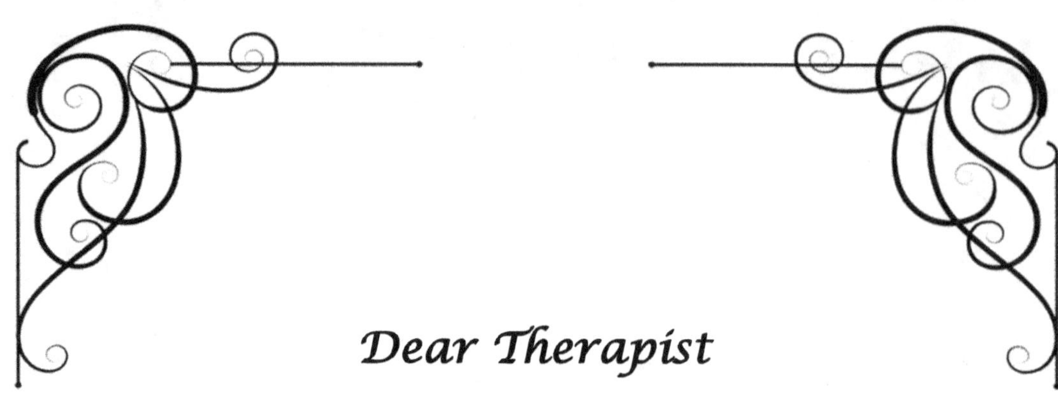

Dear Therapist

Do I let you in?
Can I let you see;
the honesty within the
one who's known as me?

The tender, hurting places; what
caused them and why.
My varied many faces and
the pulse that makes them cry.

Just thinking of your canny gaze, stings
throughout my soul, but
I'm lost within myself made craze;
cannot see myself as a whole.

I'm so afraid you'll laugh at me;
of course, not when I am there.
Just when you know I will not see.
You would not, you'd never dare.

You'd cover up your wounding ponders so
I would never know.
The feelings, laughter, doubts, and wonder,
must not ever show.

You know that I would fall and weep;
forever run and hide.
A safe place where I'd be asleep,
with no wish to confide.

It's not only you might laugh at me;
there's more behind this fear.
It's dangerous to let you see,
how I formulate my tears.

I've been crushed and broken.
I'm not really all that smart.
Protection wants to stay unspoken;
hiding mute within my heart.

I've walked along this path before
and met with lies and shame.
Other times I've opened up my door
and in the devil came.

But alas, I'm lost.
I cannot find a way, to
deal with all that's in the past and
carry on another day.

Trust

Broken, blackened, bleeding;
searching out I found your hand.
I long desperately for healing.
You say you want to understand.

You make offers that I've heard before
and speak truths which I have held.
It's tender care, I'm wanting more.
Still, there's doubt inside my shell.

Desire to go forward,
also fear what it will bring.
Secrets hold the password.
Can I trust enough to sing?

Dissociation

I am,
"Not Otherwise Specified".

I breathe,
though they say I'm not alive.

I have my own name.
But I'm told I'm not a person.

I'm lonely.
Though, I am not actually real.

You gaze into my eyes,
while you're looking at her face.

You talk together with her,
while I sit still and listen.

You seek her,
then I'm sent to the attic.

Your hand spoons hers,
while you are not touching me.

She mother's your children,
when I babysit.

We are like sisters,
with only one body.

Truly now;
what do you think?
Is she crazy
because of Me?

Love Starved Child

Tender, concerned, caring attention,
magnetizes the needy child.

Warmth melts the barricade.
The aggrieved one cautiously creeps out.

The hungry stand hoping for
portions of milk and honey.

Searching through benevolence,
like looking for a prize in a cereal box.

Can the treasure be found in all
the sugar-coated morsels?

In spite of all the goodness,
hope shrinks back from where it came.

Falling, falling, falling;
back to the place she calls her home.

Can't look kindness in the face
when it calls her name again.

Seeing only what seems to be a mask;
a gem coated shell for a heart.

It finds her wasting with hunger,
then fills her with emptiness.

She hides her eyes and covers her face,
so no one sees her tears.

She sends someone taller, stronger,
to face the world she hides from.

Someone who can laugh and tease;
know exactly how to please.

Someone to look like her,
but be someone else.

She lives within her sorrow.
It's become her faithful friend.

She and her companions;
safe within.

To venture out will only
dish out hurt again.

Crumbs of Her Bread

She forms with her hands what she
sees in her mind.
She has sparkling eyes.
She's one of a kind.

With this beautiful backdrop,
I enter stage right.
Beneath this fair picture,
I don't feel quite right.

She calculates numbers and
makes her own clothes.
She can make beauty out of
rubble and stones.

My head's full of nonsense,
not clear who I am.
So guilty and stupid,
I followed a scam

She's light on her feet;
Dances always with grace.
With long, lovely hair,
adorning her face.

I'm clumsy so stumble,
my way to the couch.
Self-conscious and giggly,
I try not to slouch.

Her beauty is pure;
clear down to her heart.
To a man, she's enticing and
she's also quite smart.

So crazy, I'm lazy,
confused, and quite numb.
Though when I try hard,
still can't get a thing done.

She cares for the sick;
always faithful to God.
Its women like her,
I bow and applaud.

It's her husband I need,
to help me learn to think straight.
He is the expert to
end my mental debate.

I pay a high price for
crumbs of her bread.
I often leave hungry, while
she is well-fed.

Oh, Little Girl

Oh, little girl,
Little girl,
Are you truly there?

There are things in
all those boxes;
you may want to share.

I watch you as you
sit and hide,
behind the attic door.

What should I do about you?
Should I listen anymore?

Do you want me to come help you,
clean up the dusty mess?

Comb your hair,
wash your face,
and make you a new dress?

Does it matter you are up there,
concealed within my mind?

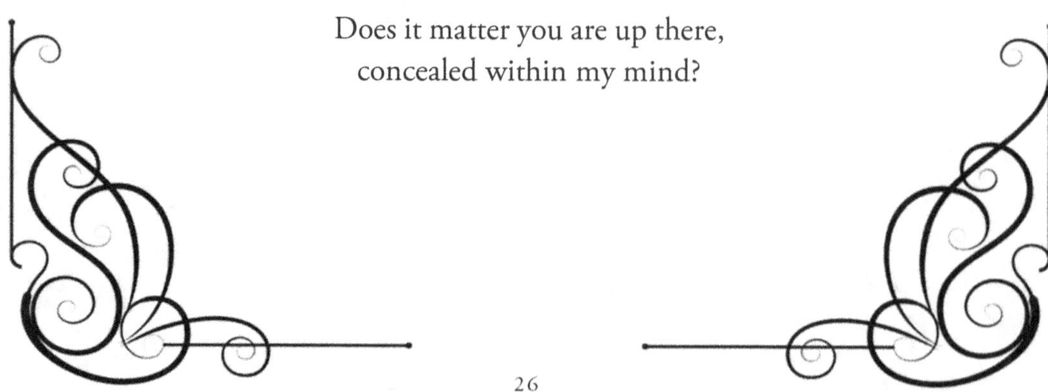

Is there something you are hiding,
that I should try to find?

Do I need to pay attention,
to your shuffles on the floor?

Should I come up there to help you,
open up that cumbrous door?

Do you want someone to listen, to
what do you have to say?

Would you like someone to care,
and let you out to play?

It seems I cannot leave you,
to always be alone.
If I walk ahead without you,
my heart will turn to stone.

Should I leave you in your tiny room,
safe within my heart?

I feel your presence baffle me.
I don't know why you're there.

As you strangely rise within me,
then hide behind my hair.

I often sense you grieving and
want to dry your tears.

I wonder why you are so young, though
you've lived so many years.

Are you someone just imagined, and
really no one real?

Should I let you have my body?
Would that help us heal?

I named you Florentina;
without really knowing why.

It just seems to fit your tiny frame;
your sweetness,
so confused and shy.

I'll wrap you warm with tenderness, then
leave you there to rest.

As I go seek and ponder,
how to help you best.

I do not know,
it's so obscure;
what am I to do?

But as you wait and wonder,
don't let your heart fall blue.

Falling

Where am I falling?
I descend, arms outstretched,
belly first, into a
voice calling from the mist.

I hope, pray for,
the softness of
a gentle heart to catch me.

Is my hope real; or a lie?
It's a question,
a compass, on a
not so merry-go-round.

Waiting Room

Sitting here thinking,
trembling through soothing music,
confined by anxious anticipation of
the sound of the turning doorknob.

Emotions,
writhe in the walls of my heart,
wanting to climb
the high dive.

Thoughts,
try to find their perfect form so
they splash down with grace
into a pool of words
transformed from tears.

Pictures on the wall,
so familiar, remind me of the questions;
how long has it been?
Will I ever see the end?

I catch my breath,
as you open the door in your quiet,
welcoming way,
to watch and listen while I struggle
to turn my perpetual loops
into some kind of design.

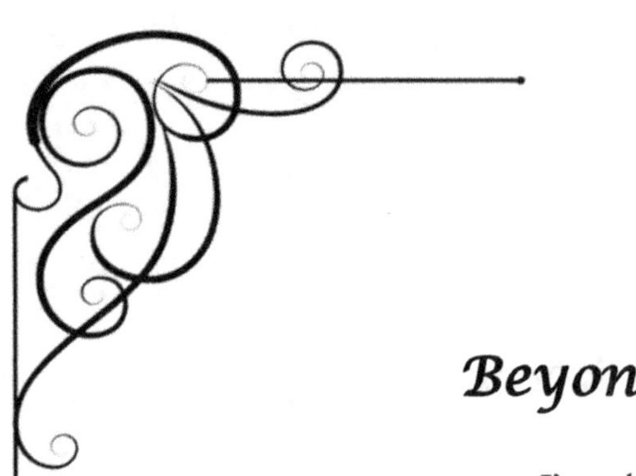

Beyond Reach

I'm where you've
wanted me to be.

You've pushed and nudged
to get me in this place.

I don't think you realize
there are blades rattling
in every corner.

My teeth are clenched,
not held by strength;
only pride with no moral substance.

You say, call then
wait for you to call back.
Press replay, the echo game.

I am where you would never follow.
The distance in your voice
will only hurt me.

I cringe to disappoint you;
if you only knew how much.
I must see beyond this place.
I've lost my ability to care about
what there is out there.

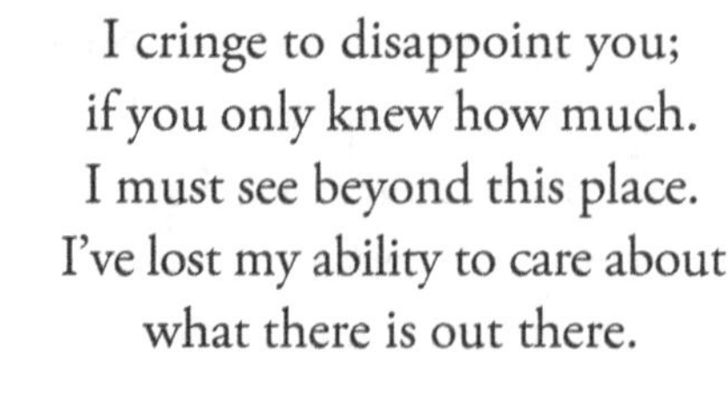

Great Man of God

Great man of God
so wise, so strong;
look down on us.
Speak your mighty words.

We are not as tall;
stand on broken bones.
Blind and lonely drifters;
incapable of lifting your mantle.

You are one who walks
on a high clean road.
Do you know things like jumping
through bushes and jagged rocks?

Your view is from above our clouds.
What you see must be much broader,
yet we know the flavor of dirt.
We see like rabbits and spiders.

God's knight in shining armor,
you are high and we are low.
Refrain from towering over us.
We get cold within your shadow.

God laid the upper trails and placed you there.
He ordained my dirt and rocks.
In His wisdom,
I am planted here.

Who am I to argue,
with one who always chooses right?
Is the truth's way always clear?
Are rocks always made of lies?

You walk steadily on your bare feet.
You have much to thank God for.
Please, don't judge;
we wear our shoes.

Foolishness

Reach back.
Search for warmth; to hold something.
If its mask unpeeled,
would it be unreal?

Call out.
Questions swirl.
Shame surrounds the number of unhealed years,
in pools of unshed tears.

I've fallen.
I taste sugar on my tongue.
Am I in a dream?
Can't tell if it exists or if it will subsist.

Caught up in a foolishness;
I wish I could believe.
Frightened to let go
of something not my own.

Walking on a razor's edge;
not knowing if the brazen truth
pressed against my heart,
would slice my soul apart

Am I living something meaningful?
Where have my pearls fallen?
Truth be known;
where have they been sown?

I wonder;
how will I live?
With no tangible answer;
without knowing
where it is I'm going.

A Child Lost

For me, there are times
things get hopelessly swirled;
with more than one mind,
torn between more than one world.

Sometimes I can be
in just one at a time;
living reality but,
I can turn on a dime.

There are many winds
in the realm I'm from.
When my progress slows,
I tilt over some.

If I lose touch with one domain,
I crash into another.
Caught by fear in the place I remain,
as a child lost from her mother.

Never To Be

Someone please,
Tell me
I'm not alone.
Tell me I'm not someone's spilled drink;
a miscarried purpose,
evaporating off the hot ground,
to be transformed into
never to be.

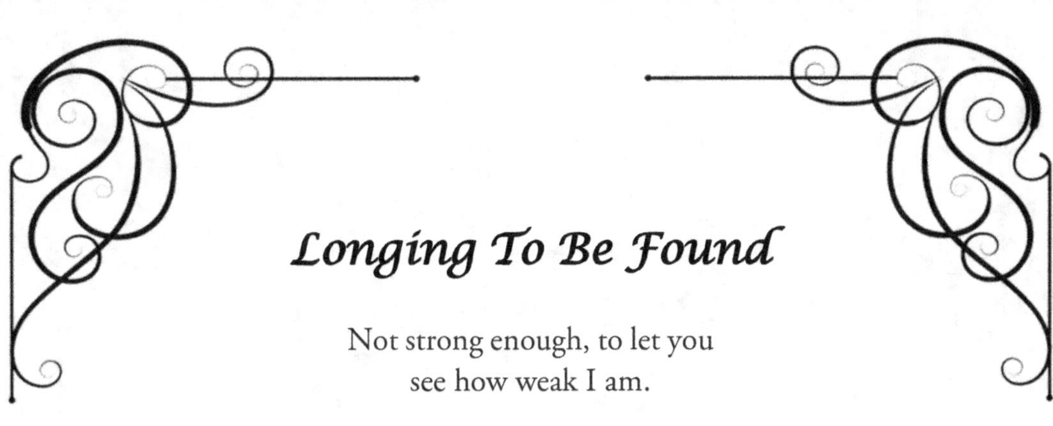

Longing To Be Found

Not strong enough, to let you
see how weak I am.

Not tough enough, to let you
know the ways I'm tender.

Don't possess
courage to tell you when
I've run away.

Fears paint pictures of indifference;
hide my garden in a blanket of dense fog;
block the light, so
I'm obscure amidst the shadows.

My heart beats strong and
hard within its cage.
Loud pounding swells my head;
surging through the entirety of my being.

I sit frozen with hope
you cannot hear;
Breathing still and
quiet as I can.

Terrified to feel
the sting of discovery,
yet wet with tears from
longing to be found.

Let Me Be

Please, just listen.
Could you try to understand?
That's all I want.
I don't want you to fix me.
Please, let me be.

I'm afraid of being alone.
I want someone to know what hurts;
to be allowed my solitude,
but not abandoned.

I was hurt when I was set apart,
without help who knew or cared.
I can only be healed alone.
God has to show me
He knew and cared.

FP

Empty Pot

Has the poetry died?
Was there no salt in the tears I cried?

Has the mystery come to an end?
Was the challenge from the need to pretend?

What does the end of the rainbow reveal?
Is the empty pot just a void that I feel?

Where did the metaphors go?
Did they evaporate, like spring's melted snow?

Is reality making me feel so sad?
As it tears me from something I never had?

Dusk

Goodbye to the sweetness
of a poignant day.

The bygone dancing heart that now
beats against the floor,
spins only memories; weeps at the door
that speaks of no return.

A precious rock;
facets from a careful hand, no longer
catch the fiery blaze,
to swirl colors on the barriers of my thoughts.

Dusk settles on a stone;
a memento reflecting only
sorrow of the passing light.

Am I Alone?

Can you sense an empty space,
growing in my place?
Do you know I've disappeared?

I am alone holding only sadness;
chilled within an echo,
as something never truly held
is taken from my hand.

What lingers in the place where
I've come so long for warmth?
I'm pressed against the door,
feeling to see into my blindness and
listen though I'm deaf.

As you hold your stick and
gently stir the embers,
where there was once
a roaring fire.

This Place

Is this a room on the bottom;
this stinging void,
blackened by no ability to feel love?
The only warmth there is
comes from the pain that makes up anger.

You'd say I'm strong, but
you can't see the nakedness that's left
when I'm uncovered;
not clothed in the ugliness
of a bloody blade.

This is where I've found myself,
cornered in a cold, sharp-edged dampness,
where I've been chased by my own effort
not to pierce and bleed away the pain; so
I won't have to see your eyes;
feel the beating of my degradation and
cringe with your recognition as honesty births reproach.

This place does not deserve applause.
I see no reason to hear my work's well done.
The rocks that jab me are made of why
I will never measure up.

What I should, do is a
rocket that will never penetrate the atmosphere.
What I wish, is a fairytale;
a child's dream covered in dust
from pages without life.

I cannot celebrate.
There is nothing laudable
about this place.

Depression

Barriers rise like car windows.
Where's the button?
What is pressing it?

Darkness fills the atmosphere.
Life transforms to struggle;
gasping through the doom.

Call through the glass.
Scream out;
a panicked cry for help.

Others watch from outside.
They hear a voice,
yet cannot understand

Switch

Flames
lit by desperation,
melt the candle down.
There's no running from the dark.
The candle flickers,
then gives up its flame.

Like the flip of a switch;
comes an alternate light.
In the middle of the night;
sun shines high noon.

Tenacity mounts.
So much can be done.
With dancing and laughter,
inspiration sparks the flame.

Kaleidoscope

Strain to see, I move deeper,
ride a slow steady train into a kaleidoscope
of broken, nonsensical impressions.
Sharp-edged puzzle pieces slice
through my heart.

Pitiless,
age-old tradition;
a journey now set in course.
No way out but through.

Try looking the other way.
What's revealed remains to
pace back then forth;
holding inevitable affliction.

Handfuls of multicolored duress
call out to draw my tears,
then pour confusion down my face.

Love in a Garbage Can

Hungry,
Longing,
Searching.

Please, see me,
love me.

Oh yes!
How fun;
delightful company.

"Come here little girl.
In here.
Just get in".

The reply;
a garbage can
With tiny white wormies.

"You're fun.
you're special.
you amuse".

Little girl's
tender heart,
broken.

Shattered,
She runs away,
but She is still there.

Can't get away;
she hides anyway.

There, where the dead dog
used to be.

Partial Pictures

Thoughts appear and then disappear,
leaving torn, partial pictures flailing,
as if caught in whipping wind,
through beams like streetlights
in the dark mist of a bad dream.

Beauty becomes ugly.
Warmth is framed in fright.
Need for love cries out.

Shards from broken images reply,
leaving infected wounds and
emotions wringing.

Pictures claim the past,
then leave me alone, polluted.
Question marks like meat hooks
slice distorted answers.

Something's Changed

I've cried, screamed, help me!
Please, someone hear me.
I need out of here.

I have trusted others to grasp visions
I believe, then find myself
doubted, placated.

Breathless, exasperated,
white-fingered, I was left dangling
over the edge.

Emotions slid into a canyon,
dug by my pleading,
through seemingly endless times,
around corkscrew curves.

Repetitive cries,
carved deep with an overburdened
history have taken my voice.

Now something's changed inside of me.
I've no more longing to share.

Close the shutters.
Shhh, quietly shut the doors
to the places where I weep.

Others can believe I'm fine.
Silence can paint a pretty picture.
Let others judge from blindness.
Allow them to believe what they see.

The one who knows all things
has been whispering to me.
He knows my strength;
compassion when I'm weak.

My desire to heal is a sweet melody.
A song He's teaching me to sing.
With His still and quiet voice,
He lets me know He is with me.

Whispers

It's a mystery
with an insatiable thirst,
to know things painfully illusive;
unrevealed.

Truth sweats,
one drop at a time,
filling a secluded well;
waiting for a time when it will
surely overflow.

What is to happen?
What's behind the shield,
protecting the heart
of the unknown?

Silently searching for treasures;
are those whispers I hear?

I long to feel truth's pulse.
Listen to all It has to say;
ride its rhythm with my resting ear.

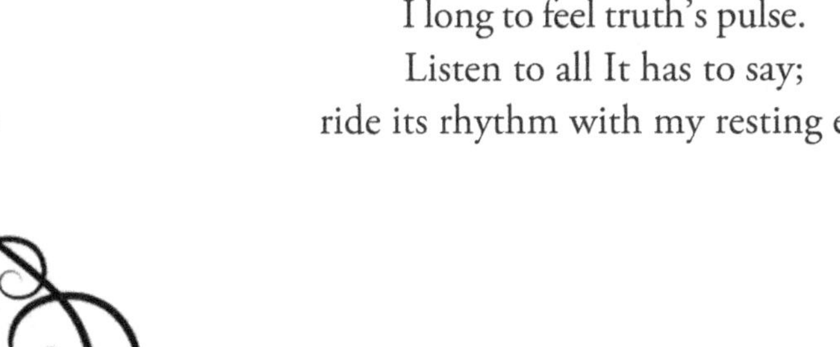

Spaces Between Words

It's simple, plain, easy to see,
dancing in front of you.
Whispering in the quiet of your heart.

A song with voiceless lyrics.
Harmony spoons melody.
A dance swoons between voices.

Blue encompasses green green drinks blue.
Sadness in their beauty
forms salty trails.

The bittersweet story is spoken
in silent oration only a heart can hear;
in the spaces between words.

A Metaphor

I want to be the only one
To tread upon a
yet-to-be-discovered field.

Where my tender souls of
unshod feet wake the sleeping earth with
warmth as fresh as spring.

I want to be the only one with
key-shaped curiosity,
to know where flowers bloom;
quench my thirst from sipping on their nectar.

I Wonder

I wonder what you'd think,
if you saw these tears run down my face.

I wonder what you'd do
if you knew what they were made of.

I wonder what you'd feel
if you knew that thoughts of you could make me cry.

I'm too afraid to know, so
I won't let you see.

I will not let my petals bloom so
you can breathe my fragrance.

Pearls

Pearls form encased in silence.
Gems from the depths,
hidden in their birthplace
until their protection is unsealed;
open to the

light as it softly pours like
luminous oil over their contours.
Revealing the uniqueness
of their warm glory.

You opened your back door
to shake out your dusty rug.
Was it your intention?
Do you realize; out came
one of your loose pearls?

It's not the kind you touch with your eyes.
Riding on air, it rang bells in my ears.
Like a seed, it Burrows deep;
planting itself in my heart.

I'm holding more than one like this.
Some escaped through holes in your pockets.
Others came to me in packages
with a fictitious return address.

They can't be held with hands.
There is no way to give them back.
They are pearls formed in your innermost being.
I will keep them in a Tender place;
safe amidst my dearest treasures.

Tiny Flower

If I gave you a tiny flower;
a pretty little weed;
Would you press it in a book?
Or let it wilt,
to be tossed away?

Where are the pearls
I tenderly put into your hand?
Do you wear them around your neck?
Or have you taken them out
of your pocket to drop in a catch-all drawer?

Kind Words

Kind words
Tickle my ribs
Ruffle my hair, then
sit quietly and
hold me.

They tell me it's ok.
Rock me;
Encourage me
Until I feel safe.

Lone Voice in the Wilderness

You speak in my hiding places
that no one else has found.

Your questions shine their lanterns.
Your words pour as sweet nourishing milk;
smooth warm and filling.

You give one gem at a time.
I put them in my purse.

polished as I turn them
in my thoughts and
wash them in my tears.

Your instinct steps with the
movement of my heart, yet
I'm invisible, so
you'll think I'm far away.

Words that come from you,
are made of woven gold and silk;
they come from an untouchable distance.

You've been a wind
through seasons and years.
There through storms, you blow them away;
sometimes blowing against me,
yet ever-empowering me forward.

Where does your Compass come from?
Do you hold it where you see it with
your eyes or does it point the way
to go from in your heart?

Your touch keeps lighting rooms
I never knew I had.
Words from you are music for my mind
to play when I'm frightened.
They are wings to lift and carry me away,
high above things that make me cry.
They let me down in firm and safer places.

Now you are woven into
how I'm made; a brightness with
the silver in my clouds.
Put there by a light designed in heaven.

Where will you be
when I can't hear you speak?
The thought trembles with my fear of losing inspiration.
Who'll know where to find me if I lose my way?

The day must come though my heart may be lead,
I will have to flex my limbs, now quivering,
to stand as I tell your peace-giving eyes goodbye,
then to walk into tears I fear.

Even when I part I know you'll still be with me.
Even though I won't see the lights in your eyes and
I can't hear your wisdom pouring through my ears.

I'll be replenished by sweet fruits from the seeds you've sown.
I will listen to your voice echo in my memories.
If I lose my way, I'll close my eyes to see where you would go.

I've dwelt all by myself secluded
in the chambers of my reverie.
There I voyaged to search for reasons;
I know why I met you,
but why did you meet me?

The Lone voice in the wilderness,
my gratitude is far too vast to be contained.
The loudness of its power is like the roaring, crashing sea.
But it's mute, so I'll pour its sweet fragility
into the songs of little birds;
it's greatness to alight with the colors of early evening skies.

Unedited

Go ahead
Let it speak
Imperfectly, like a soul
Trying fitfully
To express itself.

Desire

This struggle to ripen,
create, unfold,
is the place where
this torment is born.

Desire anesthetized by life,
sleeps deep, yet does not die.
It wakens to war standing
In quicksand.

Melancholy cries for help
amidst a crowd of
deaf listeners.

Passing through the wall,
faith whispers.
God hears;
speaking of a day to come.

Stuck

Take your foot off the gas.
Girl, quit spinning
your wheels in circumstance.
Face it, accept it,
you're stuck in this place,
as you have been,
more times than
over and over again.

Never To Be

Someone please, tell me
I'm not alone.
Tell me I'm not someone's spilled drink;
a miscarried purpose,
evaporating off the hot ground;
something transformed into never to be.

Angels Will Find Me

Almost forty-seven,
yet still spinning.
Confused, after hard living, fear,
rivers of tears, and dances with mirth.

Lost somewhere in life;
not able to tell where
truth parts with make-believe.
The person I am seems distant from me.

It's silly and childish;
a grown woman like
a wayward, teenage girl.

My head shakes its own absurdity,
slapping itself with open-handed
ridicule to make some sense of me.

I want to grow up to be
captain of my own vessel.
Can't seem to fix my own compass so
I'll know which way to turn.

Ah, yet again,
faith speaks softly.
Angels will find me.
Jesus will use me like a thread.
He'll weave me into His royal fabric.

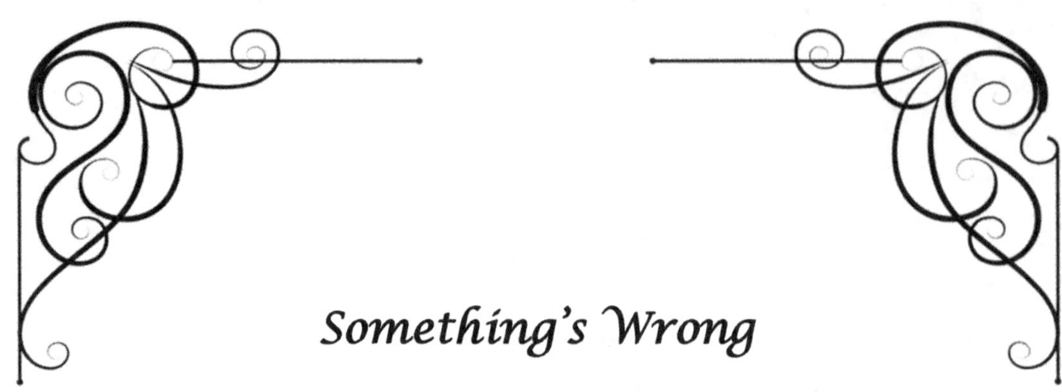

Something's Wrong

Sunshine, blue skies,
colorful flowers, and beautiful songs.
Twittering birds and the
wonder in children's eyes.

What others see so easily,
I force myself or make-believe.
Their reward is blessings.
Mine helps me crawl from under guilt.

I look happy,
talk cheerfully, and laugh.
I cover up; tuck away an
undefinable something wrong.

I want to be strong and
block out the shame of being weak.
I fear disappointing others.
I'm melting under lights that threaten
to expose me to critical eyes, so

I hide from the world
all that I can.
I falter when I try
to carry all it demands.

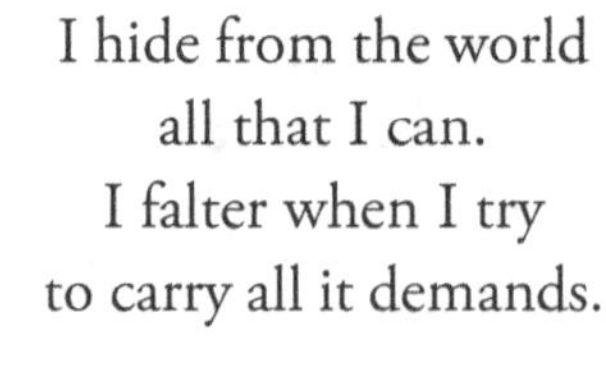

I Fall

Full of hope,
the dreamer dances.
Imagination's wings are lifted
by inspiration's currents in the air.

Soaring, I breathe in
the wonders of God's
creative hand; the heights,
depths, colors, and designs.

I see streams.
I thirst to drink from; meadows
my toes yearn to touch.
I long to swim in
emerald and blue waters.

Whipping winds from nowhere,
catch my feathers; send me spinning
out of my happy flight.

Flailing, I fall. I descend like an ax,
cutting a painful slice through all the glory.

Blood of grief coats me
as I'm stopped by my powerlessness.

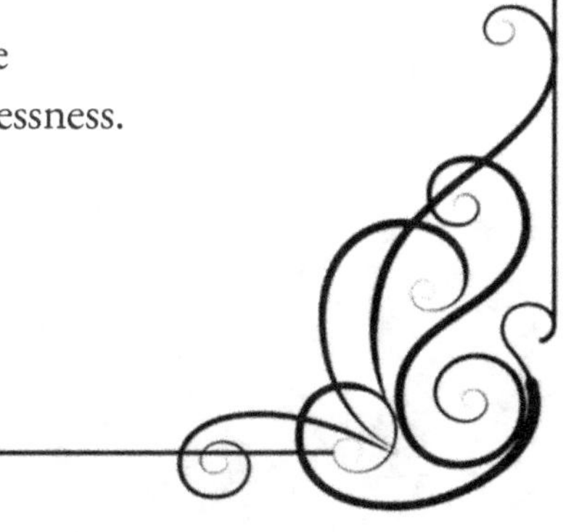

So, I Wait

Wide open space;
footpaths leading as many places
as to almost everywhere.

I stand wondering;
not knowing where to go.
So I wait.

Surely the wind will blow through my hair.
Shall I follow its kisses on my cheek; or
let my tresses point the way to go?

Can't untie the blindfold wrapped around my mind.
Turn this way. Spin around to that.
Reach to touch the sounds.
Stretch forth, then left.
If only I knew to grasp what's right.

Little Cotton Heart

What do you mean, Angel?
From where have you come?
What feeling lifted your wings when
you flew here to be with me?

I know you have come to carry a message.
What delicate morsel are you holding
in the sweet silence of your
little cotton Heart?

I wish I could feel the truth.
I want to be cradled in it.
I want to feel its whisper in my ear.
Let it melt my hurts and fears;
transform them into warm
honey and butter.

Sweet angel I love you.
You are my treasure though
you are always without words.

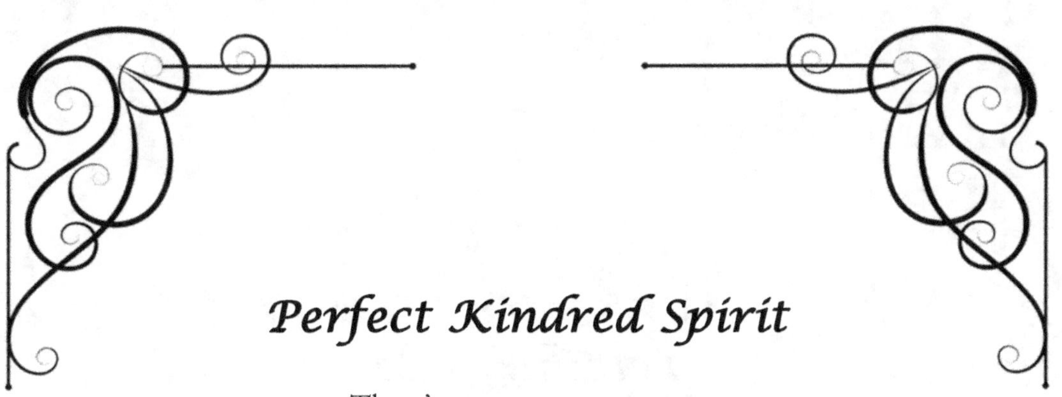

Perfect Kindred Spirit

There's no way to penetrate;
escape through boundaries that won't break.

Impossible to crash through what can't be seen.
Loneliness retreats to watch from its own world.

In the quiet, through the tears,
many lessons can be learned as truth pours
its salt into wounds.

Reality is a master sculptor;
carving desires off dreams till
they're misshapen, bleeding, sore.
In the pain of such condition,
I cringe far too much to move.

Aloneness can be not so lonely,
while amidst its mourning.
Not as fast as very slow,
dreams embrace their transformation.

Still caught within unbreakable,
outside can't hear within.
Alone finds a wonderful friend
surely sent by God.
Solitude; a perfect kindred spirit.

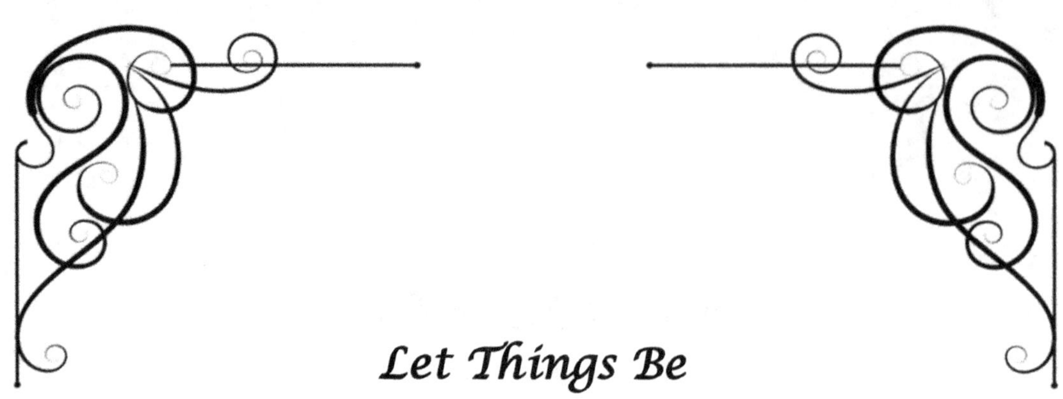

Let Things Be

I would love to be a writer someday;
who can often be found
carving souls out of clay.

Something inside me
is longing to grow.
I'll sit quiet and still,
till it's safe to be known.

I'm tired of feeling sick,
weary and numb.
Pressures crumble my dreams.
There's no way to run.

I hope there's a reason
for me to be sad.
Make a rubble of dreams,
a sweet garden path.

For now I will try not to
fight quite so hard. While
God holds my spirit,
let things be as they are.

Put Into Words

My thoughts, my feelings,
put into words, are like flowers
cut from their plant.

I can give them away;
make a stunning bouquet.
Place them in a vase;
surely to fade then wilt.

For now, I would rather let them shine
their vibrant colors in solitude,
then to speak them, and risk
finding them cast to the floor.

Secluded

My words are like rain
evaporating before reaching the ground.
Poetry gives them to angels
who carry them to a kindred spirit,
living in another place, another time.

I am seawater in a freshwater pond.
A stranger to those familiar.
A loaf of bread; others seek my crust.

I've found myself lost.
I've lost myself where I've been found.
A puppet with daydreams and schemes;
imagining myself without strings.

To be alone is
Happiness, tranquility;
a pirouette of within and without.

None can push me away.
I'm already gone;
secluded from the blur of humanity.

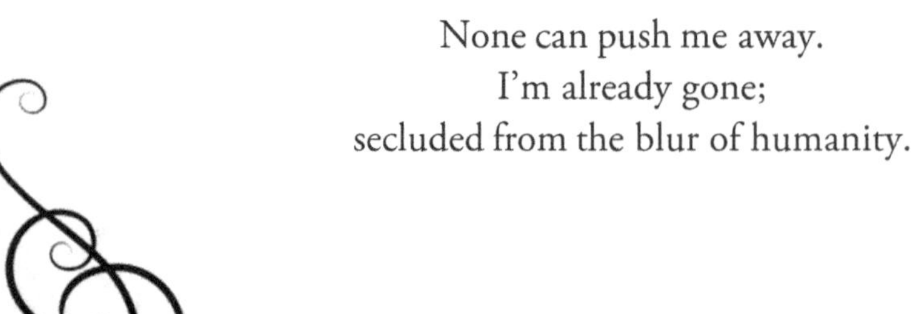

Waiting

Standing in the night on a dead-end street.
Resonating aloneness in my self-imposed isolation.

Stiffened by fear to call for help;
too insecure and unbelieving.

Hot, salty tears, trails of longing; help please come.
Heaven send truth from someone's heart.

I'm waiting in the night on a
lonely, dead-end street.

Let Go

It's about time to taste things that were not
there; to know paths, tears carved;
a broken heart's forgiveness.

It's about standing up,
learning to find the courage to release spoonfuls,
warm, filled with sweet encouragement.

It's about growing up;
learning to let go of ghosts, shapes
filled with lovely things; specialness lost, never truly held.

It's about time to find deep,
undiscovered dreams, know them well,
then bend to lay them at His feet.

Sanctuary

In my sanctuary
warm, comfortable, quiet;
soothed by the glow and
soft crackling of the fire.

God is with me,
listening to my thoughts,
patient, tenderly working
to comb away the tangles in my heart.

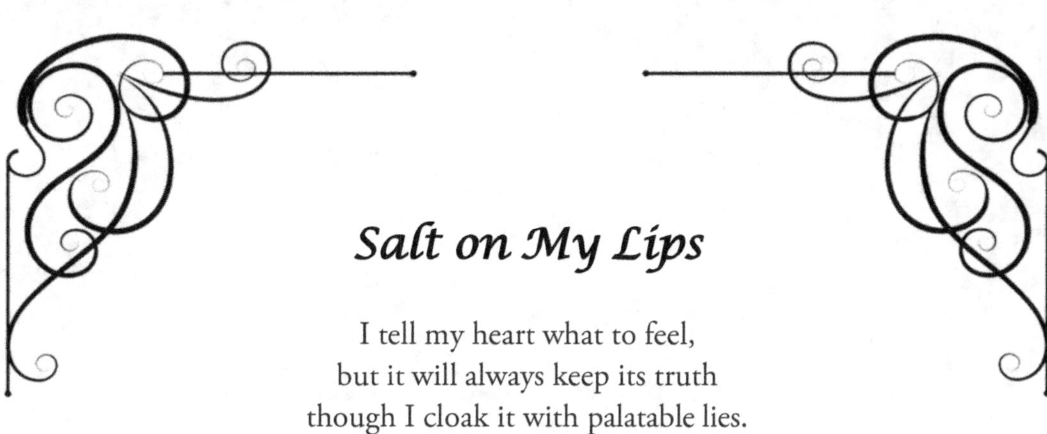

Salt on My Lips

I tell my heart what to feel,
but it will always keep its truth
though I cloak it with palatable lies.

It beats its fists;
cries beneath its cover;
throwing itself against it's locked door.

Tears, simmered in helplessness,
pave warm trails down my cheeks.
Truth leaves salt on my lips.

I lay helpless in the lap of God,
cold, trembling with fear. Will He push me off?
I've told my heart too many lies.
It will not listen anymore.
It keeps its own voice.

I don't want to embrace its rhythm.
Its unbridled affections pound conflict.

I turn myself in;
hold my wrists to receive their cuffs.
To willingly be placed in custody;
feel the texture of confinement.

Hungry, thirsty affection
does not want to dine alone,
but this time it must; sitting in the company of ghosts.

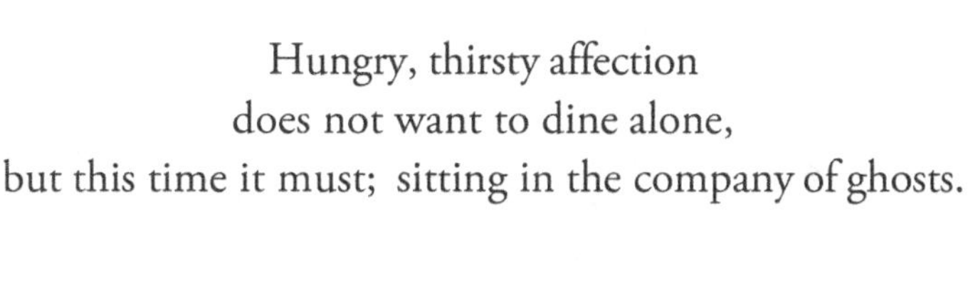

The Truth

Pretend,
Make something porous, not all it could be;
look tall, strong, as if immovable.

Something majestic, with power as ocean waves
crashing against rocks;
become silent.

Needing; compelled to
make things different than they are.

Truth stands huge as a deep-rooted tree;
helpless to be other than what it is.

Truth sits quietly, in a garden where
gifted hands care for all that grows there.

Catch Me Should I Fall

I've traveled a perilous journey over a
long, winding, scary road.

I've come to a resting place;
quietly seated on a melancholy watch;

on a path where I've crawled over rocks
washed with tears, through a black wilderness,
where fingers were my eyes.

I've crossed bridges high above ravines,
swaying in the winds, held by fibers
too thin to see; over fears that
waited open-armed to catch me should I fall.

God's Vessel

Something got jolted off its high shelf.
It fell awfully hard.
Now it's shattered, you see.

So, it's not what's believed it
could ever become the same sort of vessel
God meant it to be.

Give it some time.
He's got a design.
He knows what to do, and
He has the prescription.

Though it seems far too hard.
You can trust and you must.
Sometime you will see
He's the king of redemption.

Treasure Hunt

Looking for jewels in the rubble.
Turning each stone, I peek underneath;
forever searching for small pieces of love.

Most I find don't dazzle with light.
They can look rather plain;
a pebble, like rocks surrounding them.

Though eyes perceive no difference,
I know when I've found one.
It makes me feel warm.

It's Nice

It's nice to be recognized.
It's nice to be wanted.
It's nice to be enjoyed.
It's nice to be valued.
It's nice to be known.
It's nice to be loved.
It's nice to be sought.
It's nice to be found.

Time's Painful Grace

There I stood,
in time's painful grace,
shivering in the cold shame of suspicion;
its leery stare piercing with
white hot ice from the trust with no fire.

There I stood,
in time's painful grace;
the blood of circumstance pooling at my feet;
naiveté buried in a guilt-soaked shroud.

There I stood,
in time's painful grace,
waiting for the fragile truth to gain its strength;
it's particles to form cohesion and
begin to construct the yet-to-be-revealed structure.

There I stood,
in time's painful grace,
my patient kindred spirit, protecting vivacities
forbearing fledgling; shining light over
contours of obscured reality,
until suspicion raised a brow to its own substance.

There I stood,
in time's painful grace,
having toiled to sow seeds from my heart;
watered with the wellspring of regret,
weeping through the seasons till the harvest.

There I stood,
in time's painful grace,
until the judges' eyes revealed
the sweetness of the latter rain.

Healing

Tender exploration through the search for revelation
in a mind so ill at ease, where only tenderness can tread.
Gazing in a mirror, only compassions hand can hold.

There's hidden truth in visions that can't be believed.
I cry into lace while clinging to my pillow.
A loneliness from out of nowhere
finds a home in a listener's soft voice.

Passion, bittersweet in weeping warm;
brings forth sadness's soft giggle.
Then in silence, like a cresting sun,
healing pierces from a distant touch, then
breaks the darkness of a broken spirit.

The unknown flies away into
a place that doesn't matter.
Questions, broken pieces; become an
endless circle of saltless memory.

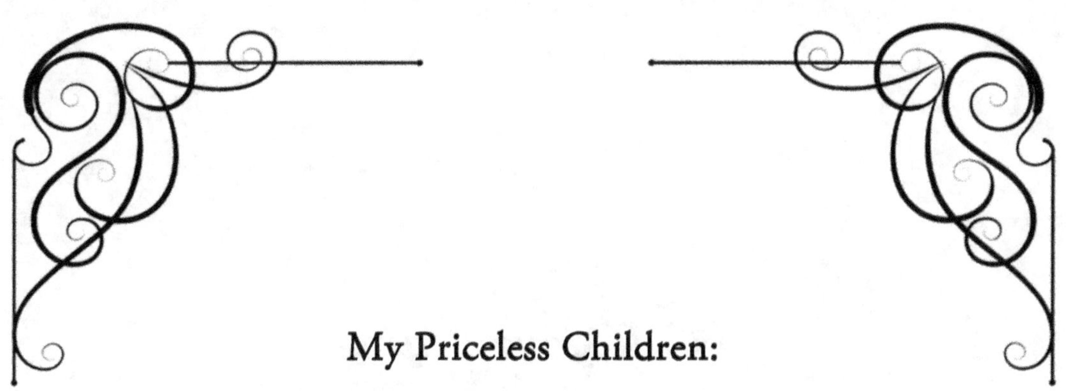

My Priceless Children:

Each one of you is a unique jewel; a gift designed in Heaven and conceived in love. You have opened your own individual places in my heart and filled them to overflowing. You are incomparable treasures that spill into my thoughts and emotions unceasingly. You are lanterns for me to see through life with prismatic light.

You have been my guide. You forged the way through jungles, being assets that have held up mirrors that reflect my liabilities. You are my courageous ones.

The love I have for you has given me the desire to face the night and gave me reasons that beckoned me forward through many years of hard days. Your smiles have been an integral source of comfort and delight to me.

Your happiness is my ultimate wish; your salvation is my loudest prayer. If I could give you what I long for in my heart, you would never feel pain, yet at the same time, I know that it is through the fire of tribulations, that you will be refined.

The pride I have in you is all to your credit. You are the ones who have chosen your paths and what kind of people you want to be. Not enough can be said of what blessings you are to me.

Yours truly, Mom

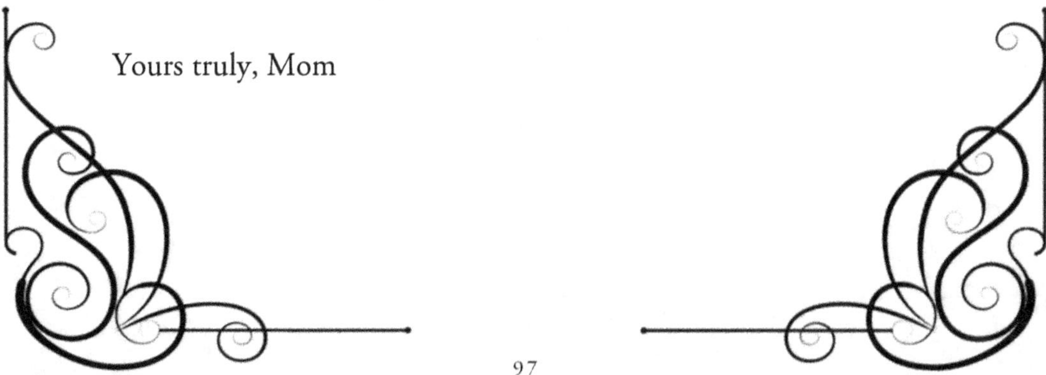

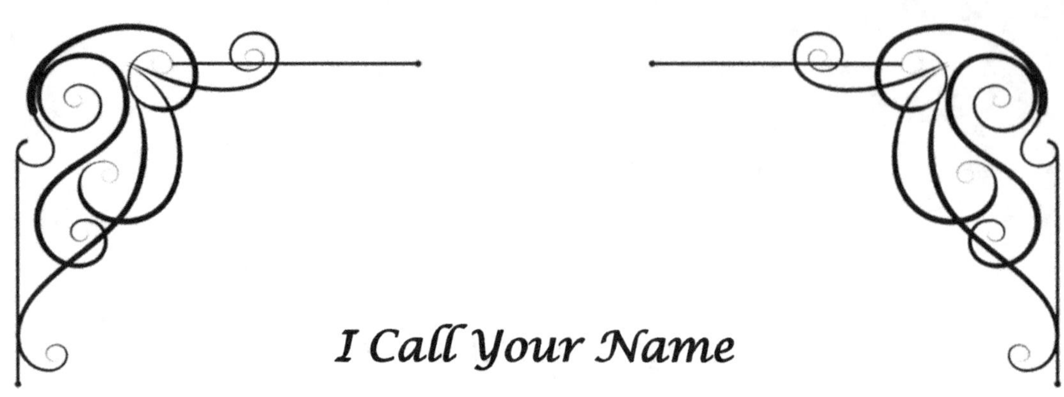

I Call Your Name

My helpless hands reach for you.
I'm pouring my heart through my fingers.
My ink is my tears.

I call your name, but you are silent.
Can you hear me?
I wonder unendingly.

Can I reach you?
Can I touch your heart?
Is that you I feel touching mine?

Oh, my son.
My wonderful boy. How I miss you.
I long to know where you are.

I yearn to know that you feel peace;
that you didn't feel the violence
of being torn away.

I want it to have been a wonderful thing for you.
I want it to be so amazing and
filled with understanding,
you do not feel pain in your loss.

I want love to be able to explain this to me.
It's hard to believe that love could
have reason to take you away.
But I want it to be love that you're surrounded with now.

In spite of your passing from this world,
I know that you're still alive.
My feeling for you is not a
phantom feeling of a lost limb.

Since you were taken away,
I have lived through countless goodbyes.
I struggle with truth and lose you
over and over again.

My feelings for you flow without end.
I never want to let go of them. They are all
I have left of you to hold.

There is no hope that
I will ever see you here again. But
there is limitless hope that we'll be together again,
when I leave here and pass through the boundary
into the world as you now know it.

Selah

Hold it all up.
Filter it through.
Float over the waves.
Rest in the motion.
Lay it all down,
one piece at a time.
Let it be, as it is.
Allow Him to keep it,
encapsulated in His wisdom.
Be at peace,
in your incapacity.

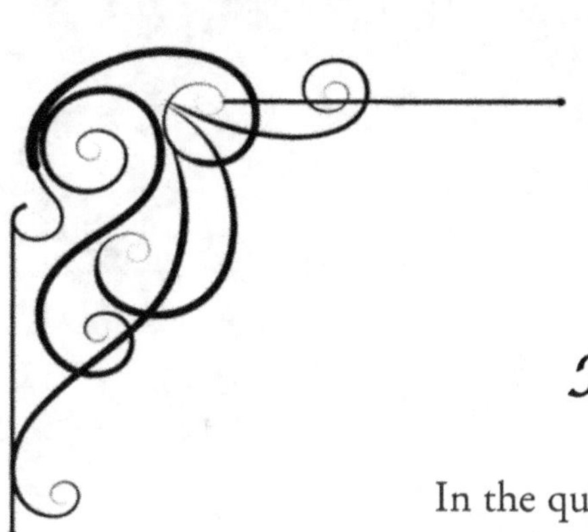

New Day

In the quiet of the dark predawn,
the roosters' crow to call the
coming of a new day.

The tap of the newspaper
hitting the front door
will open to the events of a new day.

The clock ticks toward the
bell of the wake-up alarm to
ring on a new day.

The coffee pot clicks on
to make the hot goodness that
arouses the promise of a new day.

Soon the household will
awaken to the light of
the sunrise of a new day.

Every being will hope
for God's blessing on a new day.

In the evening,
pillows will beckon the sleepers who
will replenish their strength,
before the beginning of a new day.

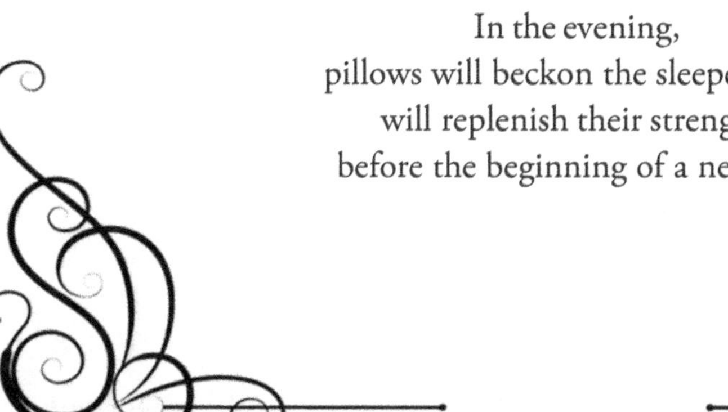

Happy Thanksgiving

Little bug
On my paper,
Flitting about;
You leave your invisible footprints,
as you dance on my words, before
you lift yourself to fly in the lamplight.

I will share
my space with you.
I give you only one request.
For your good as well as mine, please,
stay out of my coffee.

USE
FRONT DOOR